POM POM
gets the grumps

PUFFIN

by
Sophy Henn

One morning Pom Pom got out of bed
on the wrong side.

And then **nothing** was right.

His blanky, Timmington, couldn't be found.

Anywhere.

"Harrumph!" said Pom Pom.

His baby brother, Boo Boo,
was playing with his favourite toy.

"Harrumph!"
said Pom Pom.

Pom Pom's mummy sang silly, soppy songs
all through breakfast.

His cereal was soggy and
there were bits in his juice.

"Harrumph!" said Pom Pom.

Then things went from bad to worse . . .

His toothbrush was
too scratchy.

His flannel was **just**
freeeeeezing.

And he couldn't do
a thing with his hair.

"Harrumph!"
said Pom Pom.

After **all** that,
it was time to go.

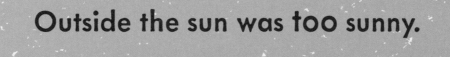

Outside the sun was too sunny.

And the birds
were too noisy.

"Harrumph!"
said Pom Pom.

"Have a **lovely** day, dear,"
said Pom Pom's mummy.

"Harrumph!"
said Pom Pom.

In the playground everyone was having fun.

Except
Pom Pom.

"Fancy a kickabout?"
asked Buddy.

"NO."
huffed Pom Pom.

"Want to watch ants?"
asked Rocco.

"NO."
grumbled Pom Pom.

"Would you like to play catch?"
asked Baxter.

"NO!"
shouted Pom Pom.

"Do you want to do skipping?"
asked Scout.

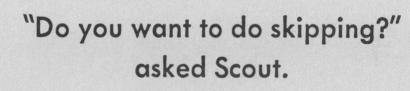

"G
AW

O AY!"

yelled
Pom Pom.

And they did.

"oh."

Pom Pom didn't feel like shouting any more.
He felt sad. And a bit silly.
His friends had only tried to be nice.

"Oops,"
said Pom Pom.

And off he went to find the others.

"Sorry, everyone," said Pom Pom.

"That's OK,"
said everyone.

"I know," said Baxter.
"Let's play chase!"

"I'll be chaser,"
said Buddy.

"Yay!" said everyone.

"Got you!" said Buddy.

"Harrumph!"
said Pom Pom.

For Rob
who almost never
gets the grumps!
x

PUFFIN BOOKS
Published by the Penguin Group: London, New York,
Australia, Canada, India, Ireland, New Zealand and South Africa
Penguin Books Ltd, Registered Offices: 80 Strand, London WC2R 0RL, England
puffinbooks.com
First published 2015
001
Text and illustrations copyright © Sophy Henn, 2015
The moral right of the author/illustrator has been asserted
Made and printed in China
Hardback ISBN: 978–0–723–29476–4
Paperback ISBN: 978–0–723–29916–5